VICTORIAN CATS

BOOK ONE: THE LIFE AND TIMES OF ROSE AND LEOPOLD

WRITTEN BY CATHERINE J. GOLDEN
ILLUSTRATED BY PAM GOLDEN

Black Rose Writing
www.blackrosewriting.com

The final approval for this literary material is granted by the author.

First printing

All characters appearing in this work are fictitious. However, public figures and customs are taken from the history of the Victorian period.

ISBN: 978-1-61296-188-0
PUBLISHED BY BLACK ROSE WRITING
www.blackrosewriting.com

Printed in the United States of America

Victorian Cat Tales is printed in Book Antiqua

Catherine J. Golden

In memory of Lee, my loyal cat and writing companion

Pam Golden

In memory of Josephine, my wonderful friend

Preface

There once lived an orange cat named Leopold of Saxe-Coburg and Gotha of Germany. Leopold heard that there were many lovely cats living in the cellar of Buckingham Palace in England. The loveliest cat of all was named Rose.

So when the future Prince Albert traveled to England from Germany to marry his first cousin, Queen Victoria, Leopold hid in the luggage. This is the story of the two Victorian cats named Rose and Leopold. As you follow their adventures, you will learn about life in England during the 1800s.

Chapter 1
Leopold Pays a Call

Leopold ran up the path to Rose's house. She lived in Buckingham Palace, the home of Queen Victoria. Leopold pawed at the cellar door and meowed, "Rose, I want to be your friend."

There was no answer. Leopold pawed again. "Rose, Rose," meowed Leopold loudly. "Please open the door. I want to be your friend."

"Are you here to visit me?" Rose meowed back.

"Yes, of course," said Leopold. "Please open the door."

"You must leave your calling card at the door, Leopold," Rose insisted. "I cannot admit any cat without a calling card."

"But I don't have a calling card," wailed Leopold.

"All my cat friends have calling cards," meowed Rose.

"I am new to England, Rose. I do not know your ways," said Leopold. "What does a calling card look like?"

Rose peeked through the keyhole and saw a handsome shorthaired cat with an orange coat and a magnificent tail. He looked eager to be her friend. "Leopold," Rose purred. "Wait a minute. I will get my calling card to show you."

Rose ran to her parlor. She returned carrying a pale pink card with pink roses above her full name, Rose Victoria, and her address. Rose opened the door a crack and handed Leopold her card.

"Leopold," she purred, "a calling card is small enough to fit into your coat pocket. A lady cat or a gentleman cat uses it for introductions or to pay a visit. All cats who pay visits must have calling cards," said Rose.

"If I bring a calling card, will you let me visit you?" asked Leopold, who thought Rose was the most beautiful cat he ever saw. Leopold liked how Rose's fur was buff and white. Her eyes were topaz like his eyes. She held her tail high as she walked.

"Yes, come back with your calling card, Leopold," meowed Rose.

Leopold ran as fast as he could to a stationer's shop. Leopold said to the shopkeeper, "Can you make me a calling card?" He showed the shopkeeper Rose's calling card.

The shopkeeper agreed and said, "What color will your card be?"

Leopold chose a card with a pale green background and a sprig of catnip. As soon as his calling cards were ready, he ran back to Buckingham Palace. "Rose, Rose," meowed Leopold loudly. "I want to be your friend."

"Are you here to visit me?" Rose meowed back.

"Yes, of course," said Leopold. "Please open the door."

"Please leave your calling card at the door, Leopold," Rose insisted. "Then I can let you in."

Leopold left his calling card at the door. Rose admired Leopold's pale green calling card with a sprig of catnip around his name and address. Rose purred loudly. She opened the door to greet her new friend, Leopold.

Chapter 2
Tea For Two

Rose invited Leopold to join her for tea at Buckingham Palace on the very next day. Leopold eagerly opened the invitation. It read, "Rose would like Leopold to come to tea tomorrow at 4:00 PM."

Leopold never tasted tea before. In Germany, he liked to drink coffee with milk. Leopold wanted to please his new friend Rose.

Leopold wrote back, "I am happy to come to tea. I will bring you tealeaves."

Rose was happy that her new friend was so thoughtful.

Leopold went to a teashop. "What kind of tea should I buy for my friend Rose?" Leopold asked the seller.

"Is she a good friend?" asked the tea seller.

"I want her to be a good friend," purred Leopold.

"Then buy her Chinese tea. It is the purr-fect quality," purred the tea seller. *This cat is not a British cat,* thought the tea seller slyly. *I can tell by his accent.*

The tea seller was not honest. He decided to cheat Leopold. The tea seller sold Leopold recycled tealeaves instead of fresh Chinese tealeaves; he had dyed the leaves to make them look like new.

He will not know the difference, the tea seller thought to himself.

Leopold did not notice the difference. He happily paid for the tea.

The next day, Leopold took his bag of tea in his paws, ran to the palace, tapped at the cellar door, and left his calling card. Rose read the card and opened the door to let in her new friend.

Rose was delighted by the gift of tea. The two cats took a quick catnap and woke up in time for tea.

"Leopold," purred Rose, "have you ever tasted tea?"

"No," said Leopold. "In Saxe-Coburg and Gotha, I drink coffee with milk."

"I hope you enjoy your first cup of tea," Rose mewed.

Leopold held the teacup in his paws. He took a sip. It tasted terrible. *It is schrecklich,* he thought to himself. Leopold mewed politely. After all, he was Rose's guest. Rose tried her tea and made a face and hissed. The tea not only tasted bad. The tealeaves left a black stain on Rose's buff coat and Leopold's orange fur.

"The tea seller must have sold you recycled tealeaves," hissed Rose. "Real Chinese tea tastes delicious and does not stain a cat's fur coat," Rose added. "I will make you a fresh pot of tea."

Rose brewed tea with her own Chinese tealeaves and handed Leopold another teacup filled with fresh steaming tea. This time, when Leopold sipped the tea, he purred. His fur did not turn black.

"I would like to take tea with you every day at 4 o'clock," Leopold told Rose.

"That would make me happy," purred Rose, "but I will buy the tea."

Chapter 3
The Wrong Flowers for Rose

Leopold wanted to give Rose a present she would like. *Last time I came for tea,* Leopold thought aloud, *Rose had pretty flowers in her room. I will bring her flowers.* Leopold went back to the market. He found a flower seller.

"I want to buy my friend Rose a bouquet," said Leopold.

"Why don't you give your friend a tussie-mussie?" said the flower seller.

Leopold chose three kinds of flowers for the tussie-mussie: scarlet geraniums, foxgloves, and poppies.

"Are you mad at your friend?" the flower seller asked Leopold.

"What a silly question to ask," said Leopold.

He paid the flower seller and ran straight to Buckingham Palace.

He pawed at the door, left his calling card, and waited. Rose found the card and opened the door. She saw Leopold standing there holding a tussie-mussie.

"A gift for you, Rose," meowed Leopold. "I hope you like these flowers more than the tealeaves."

"How lovely these flowers look," said Rose.

She took the tussie-mussie and smelled the flowers. "How nice these flowers smell," meowed Rose. Then Rose took a close look at the flowers and wailed loudly, "Oh, no! Leopold, the bouquet has scarlet geraniums, foxglove, and red poppies."

"What have I done now?" he asked Rose. She gave Leopold back the flowers, hissed softly, and shut the door without saying goodbye.

Chapter 4
The Victorian Language of Flowers

Leopold ran straight back to the flower seller. "When I bought flowers for this tussie-mussie," meowed Leopold, "you asked me if I was mad at my friend. Why did you ask me that?"

The flower seller said, "Every flower has a meaning. Don't you know the language of flowers?"

"No, I do not," meowed Leopold. "Can you teach me?"

"Well," said the flower seller. "A scarlet geranium means stupidity. Why did you choose a scarlet geranium? And why did you choose a foxglove?"

"I chose a foxglove for its purple color. It is a pretty flower. What does a foxglove mean?" asked Leopold.

"A foxglove means insincerity," replied the flower seller. "And a red poppy means sleep and death."

Leopold was very embarrassed. He began to groom himself. Victorian cats, like cats today, do that when they are embarrassed. "I was trying to tell Rose that I want her to be my special friend," meowed Leopold.

"The geranium and foxglove told her she is stupid and insincere," said the tea seller. "The poppy said her friendship is so deadly, it put you to sleep," added the flower seller.

"I am a German cat," mewed Leopold, "and I do not know English ways. Please help me choose flowers that will show Rose I want her to be my special friend."

The flower seller agreed.

Leopold ran back to the palace with his new tussie-mussie. He pawed at the cellar door, left his calling card, and waited for Rose to open the door.

Rose found the card and opened the door. She saw Leopold standing there holding a tussie-mussie. "A gift for you, Rose," meowed Leopold. "I hope you like these flowers more than the other bouquet and the tealeaves."

"How lovely these flowers look," said Rose. She smelled the flowers. "How nice these flowers smell," meowed Rose. Then Rose took a close look at the flowers and purred happily.

A proud Leopold purred back, "The daisies mean innocence; my love for you is pure. Bluebells mean constancy; I am loyal to you. And the red roses mean I love you."

Rose told Leopold: "Now you know the language of flowers."

The two cats held paws. The tussie-mussie was by their side. They smelled the flowers together. They drank tea together. They admired each other's calling cards. And then they climbed into Rose's basket together. It was time for a catnap.

Rose and Leopold were becoming the best of friends.

Epilogue

The Victorian period marks the dates when Queen Victoria reigned: 1837-1901. Queen Victoria married Prince Albert in St James's Palace on February 10, 1840. Prince Albert learned about British life and taught Queen Victoria some German customs. In the Victorian cat tales to come, you will learn more about the life and times of Victorian England and their royalty, Queen Victoria and Prince Albert, as well as the cats living in the basement of Buckingham Palace, Rose and Leopold.

Glossary

Victorian Age: The dates when Queen Victoria reigned: June 20, 1837 - January 22, 1901.

Queen Victoria: Born on May 24, 1819, Victoria, the longest reigning British monarch, was the daughter of Prince Edward, the Duke of Kent and Strathearn, fourth son of King George III. Her mother was the German-born Princess Victoria of Saxe-Coburg-Saalfeld. Victoria inherited the throne at age 18 after the deaths of Princess Charlotte of Wales (the daughter of George IV), her own father, and his three elder brothers.

Prince Albert of Saxe-Coburg and Gotha: Born August 26, 1819, Prince Albert was Queen Victoria's first cousin. They married on February 10, 1840 and had nine children. A noted reformer, Albert died of typhoid fever on December 14, 1861; Victoria and her nation went into deep mourning.

RSPCA: Founded by a group of 22 reformers in 1824 and originally named the Society for the Prevention of Cruelty to Animals (SPCA). Queen Victoria was very fond of animals. Victoria had many dogs in her household. She also had a favorite Angora cat named White Heather. In 1840, she renamed the first ever animal welfare charity (SPCA) the Royal Society for the Prevention of Cruelty to Animals (RSPCA). Today it has branches in England and Wales. The RSPCA inspired the founding of other animal charities including the American Society for the Prevention of Cruelty to Animals, the ASPCA, a non-profit animal charity founded in New York in 1866.

Buckingham Palace: The official residence for the reigning British monarch with Queen Victoria's accession to the throne in 1837.

calling card: A small rectangular-shaped card that a lady or gentleman uses for introductions or to pay a visit. Professional business cards that people use today resemble Victorian calling cards.

stationer's shop: Where Victorians bought writing paper and envelopes. Today we can buy writing materials in many places, but a greeting card shop is similar to a Victorian stationer's shop.

Glossary

Chinese tea: A precious commodity in Victorian England. People kept tea in locked tea boxes. Chinese tea was the most expensive and flavorful, and the British even went to war with China for trading the Chinese illegal opium (grown in British India) for Chinese tea.

schrecklich: A German word that means awful or terrible tasting. It is an expressive word with a harsh sound to match its definition.

tussie-mussie: A small bunch of flowers presented as a gift. Although a tussie-mussie dates to medieval times, in the Victorian period, it became very popular as a fashion accessory. It could be worn on a dress or displayed in a small vase. Many tussie-mussies include flower symbolism from the Language of Flowers, so the sender could convey a secret message to the receiver.

Language of Flowers: A nonverbal language very popular in Victorian times. Each flower conveyed a specific meaning. Kate Greenaway's *Language of Flowers* (1884) is still an important source for Victorian-era flower meanings. The color or variety of the flower often changed the meaning of the flower; for example, in Greenaway's book, a red rose means love, but a yellow rose means jealousy. Here are the meanings of the flowers in the two bouquets Leopold gave to Rose:

Bouquet #1
foxglove: insincerity
scarlet geranium: stupidity
red poppy: sleep and death

Bouquet #2
daisy: innocence and purity
bluebell: constancy
red rose: love

Credits
Camello Photo

Period images in public domain

http://en.wikipedia.org/wiki/File:Old-Covent-Garden-Market,-1825.jpg

http://en.wikipedia.org/wiki/File:Pynequeensbreakfastroombuckinghamhouse_edited.jpg

http://en.wikipedia.org/wiki/File:Pynequeensbreakfastroombuckinghamhouse_edited.jpg

http://posy.typepad.com/posy/photographs_of_march_2008/

http://upload.wikimedia.org/wikipedia/commons/a/a1/Franz_Xaver_Winterhalter_Family_of_Queen_Victoria.jpg

Catherine J. Golden has a passion for Victorian culture and cats. *Victorian Cat Tales* joins her twin interests. She teaches courses on Victorian literature and children's literature at Skidmore College.

She is a professor of English and the award-winning author of *Posting It: The Victorian Revolution in Letter Writing.* She also wrote a book titled *Images of the Woman Reader in Victorian British and American Fiction* and edited five collections. She lives in Saratoga Springs, New York.

Pam Golden is a sculptor and art educator. She works with clay and mixed media to create sculptures and sculptural installations.

You can visit her website at www.pamgolden.com. She lives in Marshfield, Massachusetts.

CPSIA information can be obtained
at www.ICGtesting.com
Printed in the USA
LVIC042158280313
326613LV00002B